In the Tall, Tall Grass

For my Father and Mother, with love

Published by Henry Holt and Company, Inc.,
115 West 18th Street, New York, New York 10011.
Published simultaneously in Canada by Fitzhenry & Whiteside Ltd.,
195 Allstate Parkway, Markham, Ontario L3R 4T8.

Library of Congress Cataloging-in-Publication Data
Fleming, Denise.
    In the tall, tall grass / Denise Fleming.
    Summary: Rhymed text (crunch, munch, caterpillars lunch) presents
a toddler's view of creatures found in the grass from lunchtime till
nightfall, such as bees, ants, and moles.
    ISBN 0-8050-1635-X
    [1. Animals—Fiction. 2. Stories in rhyme.] I. Title.
PZ8.3.F6378In 1991 [E]—dc20   90-26444

First edition
Printed in the United States of America on acid-free paper. ∞
10 9 8 7 6 5 4 3 2 1

In
the Tall, Tall Grass

Denise Fleming

Henry Holt and Company • New York

In the tall, tall grass...

caterpillars lunch

dart, dip,

hummingbirds sip

strum, drum,

bees hum

crack, snap, wings flap

pull, tug, ants lug

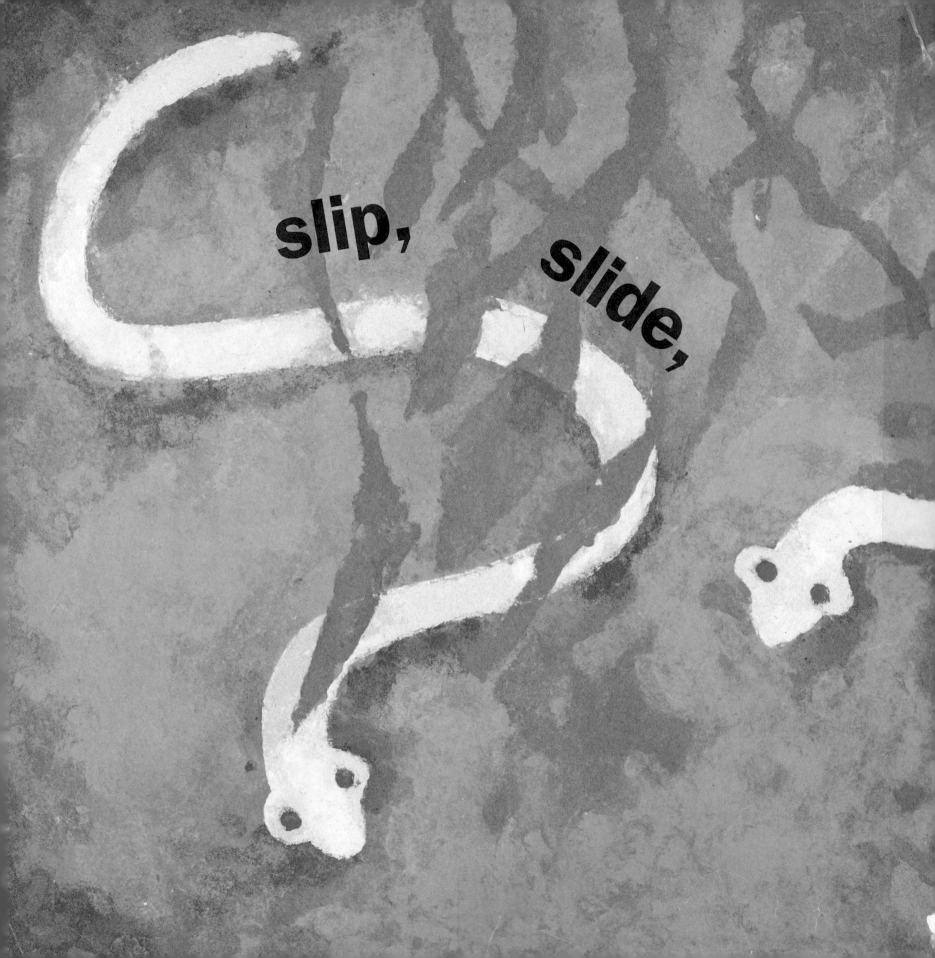

slip,

slide,

snakes glide

scratch

skitter, scurry,

beetles hurry

tongues

snap

hip,

hop,

ears

flop

stop, go,

fireflies glow

lunge,

loop,

bats

swoop.

Stars bright,

moonlight...

good night,
tall, tall grass.